About the Author

Beverley Birch grew up in Kenya and first came to England, where she now lives with her husband and two daughters, at the age of fifteen. After completing an MA in Economics and Sociology, Beverley became an editor at Penguin. Within a few weeks she was offered the chance to work on children's books and has been involved in children's publishing – as both editor and writer – ever since.

She has had over forty books published, from picture books and novels to science biographies and retellings of classic works. All her titles have received critical acclaim and her work has been translated into more than a dozen languages. Her latest novel for teenagers, *Rift*, was published in 2006.

Shakespeare's Tales

Julius Caesar

Retold by Beverley Birch

Illustrated by Peter Chesterton

WAYLAND

For my mother, with love

Text copyright © 1988 Beverley Birch
Illustrations copyright © 2006 Peter Chesterton

First published in *Shakespeare's Stories: Histories* in 1988 by
Macdonald & Co (Publishers) Limited.
This edition first published in 2006 by
Wayland, an imprint of Hachette Children's Books

Cover and text design: Rosamund Saunders

Hachette Children's Books
338 Euston Road, London NW1 3BH

Printed and bound in the United Kingdom

ISBN-10: 0 7502 4962 5
ISBN-13: 978 0 7502 4962 1

The Cast

Julius Caesar - ruler of the Roman Empire

Calpurnia - his wife

Brutus

Cassius

Mark Antony

Octavius Caesar

A soothsayer - who foresees the future

Rome awaited the mighty Caesar, its streets and squares seething with citizens eager to hail a leader's triumph. And Caesar was no ordinary leader. He had defeated the rival general, Pompey. He had fought off the threat to his supremacy from Pompey's sons. Now Julius Caesar held undisputed sway in Rome: dictator for life, commander of the Roman army, the most powerful man in all the ancient world. He ruled unchallenged.

But there were those in Rome who did not celebrate. They mourned great Pompey's loss and loathed to see the people who had rejoiced at Pompey passing through the city, applauding now at Caesar's triumph over Pompey's blood. Decked out in holiday

7

clothes, Rome's people poured into the streets to strew the ground with flowers and decorate the statues in Julius Caesar's honour.

It seemed the citizens of Rome were ripe to applaud any leader's triumph …

Into the streets strode Caesar, flanked by smiling senators and borne along amidst a jubilant mob of people, to shouts and cries of merriment and trumpets heralding the running race through Rome in celebration of this feast day.

The runners poised to begin. Caesar gave the signal. There was a joyful flourish from the trumpets.

'Caesar!' a voice shrilled above the trumpet's song. 'Caesar!'

Caesar paused. 'Who calls? I hear a tongue cry "Caesar!" Speak, Caesar is turned to hear.'

Again the wailing cry, shriller than any trumpet's note, 'Beware the Ides of March ... '

'What man is that?' demanded Caesar. 'Set him before me; let me see his face.'

A flurry of movement amongst the crowd: a man fell forwards, stumbling before the dictator. He was old, and bent, and lined. He raised his eyes to Caesar's, and in them was the haunted look of one who gazes painfully into the future and reads the fates of men.

'Speak once again!' commanded Caesar.

'Beware the Ides of March!' the old man's cry pierced the restless hubbub of the crowd ... and suddenly there was a hush. The Ides of March: the fifteenth day of March. Today was already the first day of that month! Now all were watching.

The silence grew, a creeping chill across the day's bright warmth.

All waited. Caesar stared into the crumpled parchment of the old man's face.

And then he turned his back, 'He is a dreamer; let us leave him: pass.' Within a moment Caesar had swept on, leaving the old man swallowed in the crowd that surged after the dictator along the narrow streets, even more buoyant on the wings of merriment than before and eager for the celebration games.

There was one senator who lingered behind the departing crowd with other thoughts to occupy his mind. With saddened eyes he watched the progress of this mighty leader along the clamorous street. Brutus mourned Caesar's rise to power as he might

11

mourn a death: but it was not in sadness at Pompey's loss.

Brutus loathed the rise to power of any single man: it was, he believed, the death of liberty. He dreamed of a glorious state of Rome ruled not by the whims and choices of a single, all-powerful man, but by the balanced wisdom of a collective senate. As he watched Julius Caesar stride from triumph to triumph as though nothing was strong enough to block his way, there was a twisting unease that clouded all of Brutus' waking hours; with the unease had come other thoughts that sat painfully within his mind, thoughts he almost dared not recognize ...

As he wrestled with his thoughts, he too was watched, as carefully as he himself watched Caesar. His friend Cassius had seen Brutus' brooding mood and knew what troubled him.

A sudden shout and the triumphant peal of trumpets reached them. Brutus started, stung from his reverie. 'What does this shouting mean? I do fear the people choose Caesar for their king.'

'Aye, do you fear it?' murmured Cassius, moving closer. He paused, then said with care, 'Then must I think you would not have it so.'

'I would not, Cassius,' Brutus answered quietly, and sighed. 'Yet I love him well.' He looked along the street towards the clamour, as though he was again debating inwardly some painful course. And then he shook the thoughts away and turned to Cassius. He looked at him curiously, as though aware for the first time of the deliberate pattern of his friend's probing words.

'What is it that you would impart to me? If it be anything towards the general good, set honour in one eye and death in the other, and I will look on both indifferently: for I love the name of honour more than I fear death.'

'Well, honour is the subject of my story,' said Cassius. 'I cannot tell what you and other men think of this life, but for myself, I would as soon not be, as live to be in awe of such a thing as I myself.' He moved in front of Brutus to bar his onward movement along the street and force his close attention. 'I was born as free as Caesar; so were you: we both have fed as well, and we can both endure the winter's cold as well as he!' His eyes glittered and his voice grew sharp with scorn.

'And this man has now become a god, and Cassius is a wretched creature and must bend his body if Caesar carelessly nods to him … '

'Another general shout,' gasped Brutus, turning towards the distant uproar. 'I do believe that this applause is for some new honours that are heaped on Caesar!'

'Why, man,' Cassius burst out, 'he bestrides the narrow world like a Colossus, and we petty men walk under his huge legs and peep about to find ourselves dishonourable graves. The fault, dear Brutus, is in ourselves, that we are underlings. "Brutus" and "Caesar": what should be in that *Caesar*? Why should that name be sounded more than yours? Write them together, yours is as fair … weigh them, it is as heavy; conjure with them, Brutus will start a spirit as soon as Caesar!'

Again he compelled his friend's attention, refusing to let him turn away. 'When was there a time, when Rome was not famed with more than with *one man*? When could they say, till now, that her wide walls encompassed but *one man*?'

Brutus gazed into Cassius' face, and then away again. He passed a hand across his eyes, wearily. 'I have some notion of what you would work me to,' he murmured. And then he seemed to gather strength, and spoke with emphasis. 'What you have said, I will consider. What you have to say I will with patience hear, and find a time to hear and answer such high things.'

He paused. Caesar was returning, drawing the joyful multitudes with him. The celebration games were over.

But on the dictator's face there was the hot burn of anger … and his wife Calpurnia looked pale. It seemed that Mark Antony had run into the great market place to end the race, and there had offered a king's crown to Caesar!

Caesar had pushed the crown away. A second time Mark Antony had offered it, and then a third. Three times had Caesar rejected it, firmly, and each time the crowd had cheered …

But Caesar had been angered by the people's glee that he refused the crown, for in his heart he wanted to be king. The heat and crush and noise of people pressing close had suddenly sickened him, and his old illness rose … There, before them all, in the great market-place, during the celebrations

of his triumph, he had plunged into an epileptic fit and fallen, foaming-mouthed, on to the ground.

Returning now along the street, he had recovered. But he saw Cassius was watching him. For a moment he returned the steady stare, and then he spoke quickly, privately, to Mark Antony by his side. 'That Cassius has a lean and hungry look; he thinks too much, such men are dangerous.'

'Fear him not, Caesar,' Mark Antony was confident. 'He's not dangerous. He is a noble Roman, and well disposed.'

Caesar shook his head. 'Such men as he be never at heart's ease while they behold a greater than themselves, and therefore they are very dangerous.' But now he shook the lingering gloom away. 'I rather tell you what is to be feared, than what I fear,' he asserted, 'for always I am Caesar!'

The night was wild, the sky blue-shot with lightning flame and thunder hammered like a war in heaven. The people talked of weird, unearthly happenings: a slave whose hand burned like twenty torches while his skin remained untouched, lions lurking around the Capitol …

Under cover of this monstrous night, Cassius gathered men to work a bloody and most terrible task: other senators who feared, loathed, or resented Caesar, and wished his power removed.

And under cover of this fuming night there were papers, forged by Cassius, thrown in at

Brutus' window. All claimed to have been written by respected citizens. All spoke of the great faith Rome's people had in Brutus and their fear that Caesar aimed to be crowned as king. There were other letters pasted on the statue of Brutus' famous ancestor, Lucius Brutus, a hero who had rid Rome of its last king, the tyrant Tarquin. So, skilfully, did Cassius take Brutus' sense of honour, his love of Rome and hatred of all tyranny, and fashion them into a net to bind him into their conspiracy.

Brutus twisted in the snare. Since Cassius had first whet him against Caesar, he had not slept. Since that moment on the feastday of the first of March to this, the Ides of March, for all those fifteen long days, his inner struggle had not ceased. Was there any other way to stop the dictator's ruthless climb to absolute power? His mind could show him none. Caesar wanted to be crowned. Once beneath that crown, how might he change, how might he use his power *against* the liberty of Rome and all her people? How might that man, feeling his unchallenged strength, lose all pity for his fellow men and become a tyrant?

Brutus knew no reason to suspect Caesar *would* abuse his power: and he had no personal cause to hate this man. On the contrary he loved and most respected him. But what might he *become*, climbing the ladder upwards? That was the question. And what must be done to prevent the rot?

'It must be by his death.' The words, once out, were no more comfortable than when

they lurked unsaid below the surface of his mind. 'Think of him as a serpent's egg which, hatched, would, as his kind, grow mischievous, and let's kill him in his shell.' Still he wrestled with the thought. 'Between the acting of a dreadful thing and the first movement, all the interim is like a hideous dream … '

'Sir, Cassius is at the door, and he desires to see you,' his servant broke through Brutus' thoughts with difficulty.

'Is he alone?'

'No, sir, there are more with him. Their hats are plucked about their ears and half their faces buried in their cloaks.'

So they had come to him: in the dead of night, the conspiracy, the faction against Caesar, cloaked in fear against discovery …

They entered, Cassius, and six others.

Only Cassius showed openly who he was.
The others huddled, hidden.

'Do I know these men that come along with
you?' demanded Brutus.

'Yes, every man of them,' Cassius assured
him, 'and all men here honour you and wish
that you had that opinion of your honour
which every noble Roman has of you.' And
swiftly Cassius drew Brutus off, to lay their
plan before him and bind the final threads
to hold him: a call once again on his nobility
and honour, to urge him out of the mire of
self-debate and into the urgency of action.

Brutus made up his mind. 'Give me your
hands all over, one by one,' he said suddenly.
No oaths to bind them to their task, he
urged, only their honesty and honour to keep
them firm … and so he shook their hands.

Trebonius, Decius, Casca, Cinna, Cimber, every one a fellow senator.

Cassius interrupted. 'I think it is not sensible that Mark Antony, so well beloved of Caesar, should outlive Caesar: we shall find him a shrewd contriver. Let Antony and Caesar fall together.'

Brutus stopped him short. 'Our course will seem too bloody, Cassius, to cut the head off and then hack the limbs, like wrath in death and envy afterwards. Antony is but a limb of Caesar: let us be sacrificers, not butchers.' He stared beyond the hideous deed they planned towards the glorious future that would follow. 'We all stand up against the spirit of Caesar, and in the spirit of men there is no blood.' If only they could reach Caesar's spirit and not dismember Caesar! But alas,

Caesar must bleed for it!

He turned with fierce conviction towards the other men. 'Gentle friends, let's kill him boldly, but not wrathfully; let's carve him as a dish fit for the gods, not hew him as a carcass fit for hounds ... and for Mark Antony, think not of him. He can do no more than Caesar's arm when Caesar's head is off.'

'Yet I fear him,' insisted Cassius, 'for the great love he bears to Caesar ... '

Brutus would hear no more of killing Antony. Morning light already warmed the sky, and soon this day to end the growing tyranny of Caesar would begin. It must be marred by no more than what they *had* to do.

Cassius obeyed. 'Friends, disperse yourselves: but all remember what you said and show yourselves true Romans!'

27

Brutus watched them go. Now the choice was made. Now, on this Ides of March, the inner war could stop. He had decided, and he had decided for the good of Rome and all its people.

Caesar had not slept that night: neither the ominous boom of thunder nor Calpurnia, his wife, had let him rest. Three times she had cried out in her sleep, 'Help! They murder Caesar!' for she had dreamed she saw his statue running blood, and many lusty Romans bathed their hands in it, smiling … She begged him not to leave the safety of his house today to go to the senate.

'The things that threatened me never looked but on my back; when they shall see the face of Caesar, they are vanished!' Caesar dismissed her fears. Nor would he let her talk of grisly sights seen by the night watchmen, or of the hideous shrieks like groans of dying men in battle which had filled the darkness of the turbulent night.

'Danger knows full well that Caesar is more dangerous than he: we are two lions born in one day, and I the elder and more terrible. Caesar *shall* go forth today,' Caesar told Calpurnia.

'Do not,' Calpurnia begged on her knees. 'Call it my fear that keeps you in the house, and not your own. We'll send Mark Antony to the senate-house; and he shall say you are not well today.'

Caesar helped his wife up. As certainly as he had said a moment ago that he *would* go, he now said, 'For you, I will stay at home.'

But the conspirators had come to fetch him. They smiled at Caesar. They smiled at Calpurnia's fears, and told Caesar that her dream was not of horror, but a vision of good fortune: the statue spouting blood in which so many smiling Romans bathed showed that from great Caesar Rome would suck reviving blood, and that great men would press for tokens of the mighty leader!

They said that on this very day the senate had decided to bestow a crown on him! If he sent word he would not come, they might then change their minds! They might think, if he hid himself, that Caesar was afraid!

Caesar changed his mind. 'How foolish do your fears seem now, Calpurnia! I am ashamed I did yield to them. Give me my robe, for I will go. Good friends,' he urged the men who planned his death, 'go in and taste some wine with me; and we, like friends, will straightway go together.'

Caesar had reached the entrance to the senate-house. Around the steps clustered eager senators and on all sides men pressed forward with petitions and requests, with urgent cries for the dictator's attention to their pleas.

Among them stood the old man who had warned against the Ides of March.

Caesar saw him, and stopped. 'The Ides of March have come,' he told him, with a smile.

'Aye, Caesar; but not gone,' the voice shrilled above the tumult, and then was lost.

'Hail Caesar! Read this paper,' instantly

another voice was raised, but in a moment
it was pushed aside by other suitors for the
dictator's ear. Urgently the first man
persisted, 'Caesar, read mine first: for mine
is a suit that touches Caesar nearer; read
it instantly!'

'What touches me shall be last served,' said
Caesar, generous in his self-denial. 'What, is
the fellow mad?' he asked, as again the man
pushed forward yelling, 'Delay not, read it
instantly.' And with an irritated gesture of
denial, he began to climb the stairs.

Thus did Julius Caesar push aside the last
remaining hand of help, for on the paper
in that hand were held the names of the
conspirators and details of their plot against
his life.

Now all pressed more noisily after him,

waving petitions and yelling above their neighbours' pleas.

Behind the thronging crowd, Cassius and Brutus mounted the stairs. At Cassius' elbow another senator appeared. He leaned towards them, low-voiced and secretive, 'I wish your enterprise today might thrive,' and then he advanced smiling, towards Caesar. In consternation fast becoming panic, they stared after him. Their plot already known and *Caesar* about to hear of it!

'Brutus, what shall be done?' hissed Cassius. 'If this be known, Cassius or Caesar never shall turn back, for I will slay myself.'

'Cassius, be constant,' Brutus calmed him. 'They speak not of our purpose, for look, he smiles, and Caesar does not change.'

The moment of blank terror gone, Cassius

breathed deep. Now nothing stood between them and their deadly task. Caesar was hemmed in by senators all talking urgently. Already their fellow conspirator Trebonius was drawing Mark Antony aside …

Last instructions whispered: 'Casca, you are the first that rears your hand,' Cassius reminded him. Metullus Cimber pushed his way to Caesar and presented his petition: a pardon for his banished brother Publius Cimber. Loudly Caesar rejected it. Brutus pressed closer and repeated the request. Still Caesar was adamant: no pardon. Cassius fell to his knees to add his voice.

Caesar, finding his decision still questioned, now grew angry. 'I could be well moved, if I were like you,' his tones boomed out above them. 'But I am constant as the northern star.

The skies are painted with unnumbered sparks; they are all fire and every one does shine, but there's but one in all that holds his place: so it is in the world; men are flesh and blood, and apprehensive: yet I do know but one that unassailable holds on his rank, unshaked of motion: and that I am he. I was constant Cimber should be banished, and constant do remain to keep him so!'

'Oh Caesar … ' came Cinna's cry.

'Begone!' said Caesar, still unmoved.

'Great Caesar … ' pleaded Decius.

'Does not even Brutus kneel to no avail?' said Caesar angrily.

'Speak, hands, for me!' came Casca's rallying cry. And then the blow.

Caesar staggered beneath the dagger's stab and lifted up his hands to feel, in disbelief.

Then a second, third, fourth, fifth … each chopped his sword or dagger down again, again, again.

And then the last.

Caesar raised his eyes in pain and shock to Brutus' face. Brutus stabbed.

'And you, Brutus,' Caesar moaned, and fell to the ground, writhed, and lay still.

It was done. Gored and bleeding at the base of Pompey's statue lay the mighty Caesar, dead.

Silence. The white chill of shock and panic freezing limbs and brains, the senate stood and stared. So fast it had all happened that even those who understood had only risen from their seats, before the final blow was cast.

Cinna was the first to break the spell. 'Liberty! Freedom!' he yelled. 'Tyranny is dead! Run out, proclaim it, cry it about the streets!'

Swiftly Brutus intervened, lest fear should push them out into the streets and turn this triumph to a spreading panic. 'People, senators, be not afraid,' he urged. 'Ambition's debt is paid.' He flung his arms out wide to encompass his fellow conspirators. 'Stoop, Romans, stoop, and let us bathe our hands in Caesar's blood up to the elbows, and besmear our swords: then walk we forth, even to the market-place, and waving our red weapons over our heads, let's all cry, 'Peace, freedom and liberty!'

'Stoop, then, and wash,' cried Cassius exultantly. 'How many ages after this shall this our lofty scene be acted over in states unborn and accents yet unknown! And so often shall we be called the men that gave our country liberty!'

They bent over the bloody shape that lay before them on the ground in tremulous celebration of the sacrifice, each man's head filled with the deed that he had done and the future they believed it bought for them.

Behind them, silent, a new figure entered the senate house, and stood regarding them.

Brutus straightened up, and turned.

It was Mark Antony's servant. He gazed at the bleeding body on the ground. He raised his eyes and spoke to Brutus.

'Thus did my master bid me say,' he said, quietly. 'Brutus is noble, wise, valiant and honest: Caesar was mighty, bold, royal, and loving. Say I love Brutus, and I honour him; say I feared Caesar, honoured and loved him.'

Now Antony's servant raised his voice steadily. 'If Brutus will promise that Antony may safely come to him and have explained how Caesar has deserved to lie in death, Mark Antony shall not love Caesar dead as well as Brutus living, but will follow the fortunes and affairs of noble Brutus through the hazards of his untrod state with all true faith. So says my master Antony.'

'Your master is a wise and valiant Roman,' Brutus' voice warmed with relief. 'I never thought him worse. Tell him to come to this place. He shall be satisfied, and, by my honour, depart untouched.' With a nod, the servant left. 'I know that we shall have Antony as a friend,' said Brutus. Would not all true Romans only need to hear their reasons for this deed, to share its triumph, to revel in Rome's new-found liberty?

Cassius shook his head. 'I wish we may have Antony a friend: but yet I have a mind that fears him much … '

And Antony was already among them. He entered fast, and seemed to have no eyes for any but the bloody bundle on the ground. He stood in silence over it, his back to them, speaking in low private tones, 'Oh mighty Caesar! Are all your conquests, glories, triumphs shrunk to this little measure?' There was a long silence and impatiently Cassius moved towards him. Brutus caught his arm and motioned him to stay.

Now Mark Antony turned, his face composed and quiet. 'I know not, gentlemen, what you intend, who else must bleed, who else is rank: if I myself, there is no hour so fit as Caesar's death hour, nor no instrument of half that worth as those your swords, made rich with the most noble blood of all this world. Now, while your purpled hands do reek and smoke, fulfil your pleasure … '

'Antony,' interruped Brutus, 'beg not your death of us. Though now we must appear bloody and cruel, our hearts you do not see. They are pitiful; and pity for the general wrong of Rome. To you our swords have leaden points, Mark Antony. Our arms and hearts do receive you in with all kind love, good thoughts and reverence. Only be patient till we have calmed the multitude, beside themselves with fear. And then we will explain the cause, why I, that did love Caesar when I struck him, have done this.'

Antony surveyed them quietly, moving his eyes across each face and bloody hand, though what was in the thoughts passing behind those eyes, no one could tell.

'I do not doubt your wisdom,' he said to them.

'Our reasons are so full of good regard, that were you, Antony, the son of Caesar, you should be satisfied,' Brutus assured him eagerly.

'That's all I seek,' Mark Antony affirmed, 'and ask that I may produce his body in the market-place, and in the pulpit, as a friend, speak at his funeral.'

'You shall, Mark Antony,' cried Brutus, generous in his renewed belief in Antony's goodwill to them.

'Brutus, a word with you,' said Cassius sharply, drawing Brutus to one side. 'You know not what you do,' he hissed. 'Do not consent that Antony speak at his funeral!

Do you know how much the people may be moved by that which he will utter?'

Brutus would hear no argument: now that the deed was done, he was exultant in his confidence that all would understand it was a sacrifice for Rome. *He* would speak first in the pulpit and give their reasons, and only after, would Antony address the crowd. The citizens would see that Antony spoke only with Brutus' permission and that the men who had killed Caesar wished him to have all honourable rites and ceremonies in death. Brutus' confidence bounded on: it would appear greatly to their credit to have won the loyalty of Caesar's friend and faithful ally, Mark Antony!

'I like it not,' repeated Cassius doggedly.

But already Brutus was giving these

conditions to Mark Antony: he could in his funeral speech speak well of Caesar but may not utter a single word of ill about those who had killed him. And he must make it clear he spoke only by their permission.

'Be it so,' agreed Mark Antony. 'I do desire no more.'

'Prepare the body then, and follow us,' commanded Brutus, and out they went.

Antony was alone. The senate-house had emptied of conspirators and witnesses to their grisly deed. Only the crumpled body of dead Caesar stayed, his blood glistening across the base of Pompey's statue, and Antony, who stood and looked at it.

It was a different Antony from he who spoke soft words of peace to Julius Caesar's killers. He felt the silence drop about the senate halls, and looked up, and on his face was carved a very different tale from that he told to Brutus.

He whispered now, and they were words only for the bleeding corpse before him, 'Oh pardon me, that I am meek and gentle with these butchers! You are the ruins of the noblest man that ever lived in the tide of times.' His voice cracked.

He dropped to his knees beside the body, and in one hand he gripped the shreds of robes, ripped bloody with every dagger's gash into the flesh of Caesar. 'Woe to the hands that shed this costly blood! Over your wounds now do I prophesy, a curse shall light upon the limbs of men; domestic fury and fierce civil strife shall harass all the parts of Italy, and Caesar's spirit, ranging for revenge

shall with a monarch's voice cry "Havoc,"
and let slip the dogs of war!'

In the great central market-place the
people waited, grimly restless. Rumours
flew from mouth to mouth, half-truths
gathered like buzzing bees, grew to
monstrous certainties, and then were flung
aside. Fear and mourning hung like a shroud
about the square.

'We will be satisfied,' the cry went up, and
became a chant that swelled and filled the
anxious air with ominous mutiny. 'Let us
be satisfied. Let us be satisfied.'

Boldly Brutus stepped among them. He
raised his hand for silence. At all costs, the
vast numbers of people pressing in the square
must be divided and then calmed. He urged

some to stay and listen to what he had to say, others to go with Cassius and hear his words.

The crowd parted, reformed to shouts and cries, as this or that citizen declared that he would hear Cassius or Brutus. 'And compare their reasons!' the shout was heard. It hung threatening above the square. Cassius, followed by a knot of yelling men, marched to another street.

Brutus mounted to the central pulpit. Below, the crowd heaved to and fro as some pushed closer, elbowing a path; the noise swelled and faded and then swelled again … and, suddenly, silence fell. All stared suspiciously at the man who had, they heard, killed mighty Caesar.

'Romans, countrymen!' Brutus raised his voice and sent it loud across the square.

'Hear me for my cause, and be silent that you may hear: believe me for my honour, and have respect for my honour, that you may believe: blame me in your wisdom, and awake your senses that you may better judge.' He paused and looked slowly around the assembled multitude. Already their sullen curiosity was giving way to something else ...

'If there be any here,' cried Brutus, 'any dear friend of Caesar's, to him I say that Brutus' love for Caesar was no less than his! If then that friend demand why Brutus rose against Caesar, this is my answer: not that I loved Caesar less, but that I love Rome more!' He paused again. Every man and woman watched. Silence reigned. 'Would you rather Caesar were living, and die all slaves, than that Caesar were dead, and live all free men?'

Across the silence, murmurs rippled: cautious voices of assent. One or two nodded openly: his point was taken.

To cement this hopeful mood, Brutus continued quickly, 'As Caesar loved me, I weep for him; as he was fortunate, I rejoice at it; as he was valiant, I honour him,' again he paused, to ensure absolute attention, 'but as he was *ambitious*, I slew him! There is tears for his love; joy for his fortune; honour for his valour; and *death* for his ambition!'

He leaned across the pulpit, staring hard into the faces of the crowd, 'Who is here so base that he would be a slave?'

'If any, speak, for him have I offended. Who is here that would not be a Roman? If any, speak, for him I have offended.'

Each question rang its insistent rhythm

across the square, and as each echo faded, the shaking heads and sympathetic murmurs grew, the rumbling mounting to a single triumphant answer, 'None, Brutus, none!'

Brutus gazed with misting eyes across the mass of Romans spread before him. How clearly, in their nobility, they understood what Brutus and his fellows had to do for liberty in Rome! And would not all right-minded people understand?

A drumbeat boomed across their heads. All turned. Into the square strode Mark Antony, with others, and between them Caesar's body. The murmurs died, stifled by the sight of Julius Caesar's death, so stark and unmistakable.

Sensing the people's shock, Brutus claimed their attention hastily. 'Here comes his body, mourned by Mark Antony: who, though he had no hand in his death, shall receive the benefit of his dying, a place in the commonwealth.' He lifted up his arms, to encompass all of them. '*As which of you shall not?*' He raised a hand again to ask for quiet. 'With this I depart; that, as I slew my best friend for the good of Rome, I shall have the same dagger for myself when it shall please my country to need my death.'

It was as though he had rung a bell to signal ecstasy. The crowd went wild. 'Live, Brutus! live, live!' the nearest cried. And farther off, 'Give him a statue with his ancestors!' And then rising above all else, 'Let him be Caesar!'

Brutus turned his head with sudden shock towards the anonymous cry: a new dictator to replace the old!

Already Mark Antony was mounting the pulpit. He reached the top and surveyed the crowd. 'For Brutus' sake, I am beholden to you,' he said cautiously.

'It were best he speak no harm of Brutus here!' came a mutter from the crowd.

'This Caesar was a tyrant,' came another. 'We are blest that Rome is rid of him.'

Mark Antony was beginning. 'Friends, Romans, countrymen, lend me your ears.' The murmuring of the crowd fell silent. 'I come to bury Caesar, not to praise him.' Heads nodded, approving this simplicity. To bury was fair; but not to praise a tyrant!

Antony continued, 'The evil that men do lives after them; the good is often interred with their bones: so let it be with Caesar.' He moved to the front edge of the pulpit, and looked down. All stood upon their toes to see. Below him lay the body, gory with its seeping wounds.

'The noble Brutus has told you Caesar was ambitious. If it were so, it was a grievous fault.' He paused again, and continued to gaze upon the corpse. 'And grievously has Caesar answered it.' It was as though the crowd had suddenly become a single watching eye, fastened like a gigantic bird of prey on Antony. 'Here, with the permission of Brutus and the rest, for Brutus is an honourable man ... ' the word lingered in the air, and seemed to pick up echoes, 'so are they all, all *honourable* men ... I come to speak at Caesar's funeral. He was my friend, faithful and just to me: but Brutus says he was ambitious: and Brutus is an honourable man.'

For a moment it seemed that Antony had finished. Restless movement rippled across the ranks, gloomy with disappointment. But in a moment he began again. And Antony's voice was louder now. 'You all did see that on the feast day I three times presented him a kingly crown, which he three times refused: was this ambition?' More murmurs, quickly dying, lest Antony's next word be lost. 'Yet Brutus says he was ambitious, and sure *he* is an honourable man. I speak not to disprove what Brutus spoke, but here am I to speak what I do know! You did all love him once, not without cause: what cause withholds you then, to mourn for him?' Uneasily, the vast crowd shifted, teetering …

And like a cannon's boom, Mark Antony's voice blasted in their ears, 'Oh judgement!

You are fled to brutish beasts, and men have lost their reason!' Trembling, he glared across the mass, his face grown white with anger. And then he seemed to shake himself, and spoke more quietly. 'Bear with me: my heart is in the coffin there with Caesar, and I must pause till it come back to me.'

Like a prowling animal now, the crowd writhed, surged a little forward, and from the silence, a muttering …

'I think there is much reason in his sayings,' said the citizen who had called Caesar a tyrant. 'Caesar has had great wrong.'

'I fear there will be a worse come in his place,' muttered another man.

'He would not take the crown; therefore it is certain he was not ambitious,' a third concluded.

Antony was speaking again. He surveyed them, measuring, 'Oh masters, if I were disposed to stir your hearts and minds to mutiny and rage, I should do Brutus wrong, and Cassius wrong, who, you all know, are *honourable* men … '

He gathered pace, 'Here's a parchment with the seal of Caesar. It is his will. Let but the people hear this testament, and they would go and kiss dead Caesar's wounds and dip their napkins in his sacred blood, beg a hair of him for memory … '

'We'll hear the will,' the roar went up, 'read it, Mark Antony. The will! The will! We will hear Caesar's will!'

Antony stood listening to the swelling thunder of the crowd. In all his thinking Brutus had never understood this populace of Rome, this fickle, changing beast, moulded now by Antony into his own brutal weapon of revenge.

'Have patience, gentle friends,' he told them. 'It is not right you know how Caesar loved you. It will inflame you, it will make you mad: it is good you know not that you are his heirs; for if you should, oh, what should come of it!'

'Read the will!' they yelled.

'I fear,' said Antony, 'I wrong the honourable men whose daggers have stabbed Caesar … '

'They were traitors: honourable men!' they shrieked.

Antony descended from the pulpit into the crowd and gathered them to Caesar's body to read the will. But first, he lifted up the bloody robes for all to see.

'Look, in this place ran Cassius' dagger

through: see what a rent the envious Casca made: through this the well-loved Brutus stabbed. This was the unkindest cut of all; for when the noble Caesar saw him stab, then burst his mighty heart … Oh, what a fall was there, my countrymen! Then I, and you, and all of us fell down, whilst bloody *treason* flourished over us.'

The final stone was cast. The multitudes seethed close about the savaged body, like a giant beast that sniffed and whimpered at a fallen friend …

And then with one gigantic cry, the fury broke. 'Revenge! Seek! Burn! Fire! Kill! Slay! Let not a traitor live! We'll burn Caesar's body in the holy place, and with the brands fire the traitors' houses!' And from the square they surged, hot with mutiny.

61

Alone beside the body, Antony breathed deep. Now was Caesar's spirit indeed alive. 'Now let it work. Mischief, you are afoot, take what course you will.' Now would the forces of rivalry for power unlocked by Caesar's death be savagely let loose!

Within twenty-four hours it was Antony, not Brutus, who controlled the city. Brutus and Cassius fled Rome. And into Rome came a powerful ally to Caesar's cause: his young grand-nephew and adopted son and heir, Octavius Caesar.

Rome plunged into bloody chaos, as Antony had prophesied. Citizens raged through the city looking for the murderers of Caesar. In their frenzy to search out their prey even a hapless poet by the name of Cinna, a close friend of Caesar's, was dragged away to death for no other reason than his name: it was the same as Cinna the traitor.

So began a vicious battle for control. In the vacuum left by Julius Caesar's death, Mark Antony, Octavius and a third, named Lepidus, seized power, ruling as triumvirs, dividing all the Roman Empire's territory in Europe, Africa and Asia between themselves. They drew up a list of those to die for treachery against Caesar, coldly bargaining life for life: their own brothers, cousins, nephews, all whom they judged guilty. A hundred senators to die.

In a world torn by the rivalries for power once curbed by Caesar's strength, the power of Antony and Octavius grew unchecked, while Brutus and Cassius, fled separately to exile, prepared for war against them.

At Sardis in Asia Minor, these one-time leaders of the conspiracy met again, each now leading the army legions they had gathered to their cause. Many months had passed since that distant Ides of March in Rome when Caesar fell. The bonds of warmth which tied them then had cooled: in the aftermath of the assassination and their hasty flight, and in this anxious mustering of arms for war, differences once hidden by their common purpose, now reared a menacing head. Each had grown suspicious of the other, and fear of their differences had sown a bitter discord.

How much more than minor quarrels

reared their vicious jaws to mangle them! The world whose liberty Brutus had sought by killing Caesar was ripped by bitter quarrels between rival factions, while Octavius and Antony marched on to greater strength. Unwilling to look for the cause of the chaos in the tangled web of their conspiracy, or in illusions of unquestioning honour and righteousness in which he had floated through the deed, Brutus found fault instead with Cassius: Cassius was betraying the nobility of motives for which they had sacrificed Caesar, sullying the honour of their cause with dubious methods for gathering men and money …

'Remember March, the Ides of March remember,' he told him angrily. 'Did not great Julius bleed for justice' sake? What villain touched his body, that did stab, and not for justice? What, shall one of us, that struck the foremost man of all this world but for supporting robbers, shall we now contaminate our fingers with base bribes, and sell the mighty space of our large honours for so much trash as may be grasped thus? I had rather be a dog, and bay the moon, than such a Roman!'

'Brutus, bay not me,' warned Cassius, incensed and hurt by Brutus' self-righteous accusations. 'I'll not endure it!'

'There is no terror, Cassius, in your threats,' coldly Brutus rejected Cassius' anger, 'for I am armed so strong in honesty that they pass me as the idle wind … I did send to you for certain sums of gold to pay my legions, which you denied me: for I can raise no money by vile means … '

66

'I denied you not,' protested Cassius angrily, 'he was but a fool that brought my answer back!' Fury mixed with a new despair, for suddenly he saw they teetered above a chasm which would split them for evermore. A dark world-weariness swept over him: 'Come, Antony, and young Octavius, come, revenge yourselves alone on Cassius, for Cassius is aweary of the world; hated by one he loves, checked like a slave, all his faults observed, set in a note-book, learned by heart to cast into my teeth!' He rounded sharply on Brutus, 'There is my dagger: strike, as you did at Caesar; for I know, when you did hate him worst, you loved him better than ever you loved Cassius!'

And suddenly they both saw the dark divide that yawned between them, and understood how close they came to plunging into it.

'Sheathe your dagger,' said Brutus quietly. Wearily he hauled at their years of trusted friendship to patch up their differences. At their peril they had ignored them when they planned the death of Caesar.

And Brutus was sicker at heart than Cassius could have guessed. He had just heard that his beloved wife, plunged deep in grief at his exile and the growing strength of Octavius with Mark Antony, had killed herself. He turned again toward his faith in Cassius and that vision of Rome's freedom which had spurred him on to what he'd done. What else was there to grasp at, as the war with Octavius and Mark Antony drew nearer? Already these two had reached Philippi in Greece.

Brutus was all for marching straight to fight.

Cassius thought differently: better to exhaust the enemy with marching, while they, merely awaiting their arrival, would be well-prepared.

Brutus disagreed. It was with the same confidence that he had rejected killing Mark Antony and insisted on him speaking in the market-place at Caesar's funeral. If they allowed the enemy to march from Philippi, he argued, the enemy would gather people to their ranks in every land they passed through …

'Hear me, good brother,' protested Cassius desperately.

'Our legions are brimful, our cause is ripe,' insisted Brutus. 'The enemy increases every day. We, at the height, are ready to decline. There is a tide in the affairs of men, which, taken at the flood, leads on to fortune: omitted, all the voyage of their life is bound in shallows and in miseries. On such a full sea are we now afloat, and we must take the current when it serves, or lose our ventures.'

As before, Cassius gave in. 'Then, with your will, go on; we'll along ourselves, and meet them at Philippi.' There was no more to say.

In his tent, Brutus sought a kind of peace, listening to the strains of music played by a sleepy servant. He read awhile, or tried to, searching the words that clustered on the page for some hint of certainty in the grim time that loomed ahead, until the room grew strangely dark, and struggling to clear his aching eyes, he suddenly froze. A dark chill had crept into the tent, making the flickering candle gutter, and a shadow moved across the gloom, formless, growing stronger, swelling grotesquely into the shape of murdered Caesar.

'Why do you come?' breathed Brutus, shivering.

'To tell you that you shall see me at Philippi,' echoed the sombre voice of Caesar's ghost.

At Philippi the rival armies met: Cassius and Brutus facing young Octavius Caesar and Mark Antony.

'Words before blows: is it so, countrymen?' challenged Brutus.

'Not that we love words better, as you do,' retorted Octavius.

'Good words are better than bad strokes, Octavius,' Brutus replied.

'In your bad strokes, Brutus, you give good words,' said Antony. 'Witness the hole you

made in Caesar's heart, crying "Long live! hail, Caesar!" Villains! You showed your teeth like apes, and fawned like hounds, and bowed like slaves, kissing Caesar's feet; whilst damned Casca, like a cur, behind struck Caesar in the neck!'

Octavius became impatient: hot words bandied were no alternative to the cold logic of brandished steel. 'Look,' he cried, 'I draw a sword against conspirators! When think you that the sword goes up again? Never, till Caesar's three and thirty wounds be well avenged; or till another Caesar has added slaughter to the sword of traitors!'

ompelled against his judgement to risk everything in this single battle here at Philippi, Cassius faltered before a sense of gathering doom. 'If we lose this battle,' he said to Brutus, 'then is this the very last time we shall speak together.'

Brutus looked long and hard into his friend's face, a forgotten gentleness between them warming the coldness of the future he too sensed. 'This same day must end that work the Ides of March began,' he murmured, 'and whether we shall meet again I know not.' He clasped Cassius' hand. 'Therefore our everlasting farewell take: for ever, and for ever, farewell, Cassius! If we do meet again, why, we shall smile. If not, why then, this parting was well made! Oh that a man might know the end of this day's business before it comes!'

That day did end the work the Ides of March began. On one flank Brutus pushed forward an attack on Octavius' force, and won. But he gave the signal to attack too early for Cassius' legions: forced into battle ill-prepared, they were swiftly overrun by Antony's troops.

Sinking ever deeper in despair, Cassius misread the signs of victory on Brutus' flank: watching his soldiers greeted eagerly by their victorious fellows, he thought that he had seen his troops vanquished by the enemy.

This was Cassius' day of birth: on this day he had entered the world, and suddenly he knew it was the day that he would leave it. Bowing before the overwhelming misery of the defeat he believed had overtaken them, he chose the traditional fate of Romans in defeat: death by his own hand. He gave his servant one final task: to guide the same sword that killed Julius Caesar into Cassius' breast.

Brutus, flushed with the excitement of his early victory against Octavius' force, received the news of Cassius' death like the knell of doom. He rushed to the body of his friend. Now that same despair which had taken Cassius dropped like a shroud over Brutus. 'Oh Julius Caesar, you are mighty yet!' he cried. 'Your spirit walks abroad, and turns our swords into our own entrails! The last of all the Romans, fare well!' he mourned. 'Friends, I owe more tears to this dead man than you shall see me pay. I shall find time, Cassius,' he whispered, 'I shall find time.'

Before the day was out, Brutus tried their fortunes in a second fight. This time there was no victory: as the light of that ill-chosen day began to fade, the remnants of his defeated force clung with him and sought sanctuary in the creeping dark of night. And Brutus, who had sworn to Cassius that in defeat he would not look for death, now saw only this escape ahead of him.

'The ghost of Caesar has appeared to me two separate times by night: at Sardis once, and, this last night, here in Philippi fields: I know my hour is come,' he whispered.

'Not so, my lord,' his companions argued.

'I am sure it is,' he said again. 'Our enemies have beat us to the pit: it is more worthy to leap in ourselves, than wait until they push us. I shall have more glory by this losing day than Octavius and Mark Antony by this vile conquest shall attain,' he vowed and rallied his remaining strength of purpose. 'Brutus' tongue has almost ended his life's history: night hangs upon my eyes: my bones would rest, that have but laboured to attain this hour … '

And as he ran upon the sword held by his faithful servant, he gasped to the man whose death had haunted him each minute since that fateful Ides of March, 'Caesar, now be still,' and died.

Victorious Antony came upon the body of his enemy, and stood looking down at it. It was the final pinnacle of his success; and yet the taste of it was, in this moment, bitter.

'This was the noblest Roman of them all,' he mourned. 'All the conspirators, save only he, did what they did in envy of great Caesar; he only, in general honest thought and common good to all, made one of them. His life was gentle, and the elements so mixed in him that Nature might stand up and say to all the world, "This was a man!"'

Octavius stood by his side. Now was the murder of Julius Caesar finally revenged; ahead lay only the fruits of victory. There was no power in the Roman world could challenge the might of Octavius and Mark Antony combined.

For the moment, at least, they stood together.